# BLACK IRISH

### A NOVELLA
### BY K.M. RICE

Copyright © 2019 K.M. Rice
Published by Wildling Spirit
Cover art by K.M. Rice © 2019
All rights reserved.

No part of this book may be reproduced, or stored in a retrieval system, or transmitted in any form by any means, electronic, mechanical photocopying, recording, or otherwise, without express written permission of the author. To obtain permission to excerpt portions of the text, please contact the author at kmriceauthor@gmail.com.

All characters and events in this book are fiction and figments of the author's imagination. Any similarity to real persons, living or dead, is coincidental and not intended by the author.

# DISCLAIMER

While some real events and locations are mentioned, it is important to remember that this is a work of fiction.

# PROLOGUE

*I know what you're t'inking; if you've read one love story, you may as well have read them all. But I can guarantee that you haven't read this one before. And it certainly isn't a tale of traditional love by any means.*

*So for those of you who choose to read on, I will say this one t'ing: if it has to be there at all, it's best that you go and find trouble rather than trouble finding you.*

# 1

The organ stopped tuning. The big hand only had two more ticks until it was beside the little one on the three. A tremor ran through Jack O'Connor's chest and he grabbed his suit jacket. There was a knock at the door and his sister Sarah stuck her head into the small side room of the church in Doolin, County Clare.

*I need a fag.*

"Jaysus, they're like a pack of wolves, so they are. I t'ink Orla's invited half of the county. I've never seen so many giant falsies in my life. Tarantulas, like."

"Falsies?" he asked as he donned the jacket. Sarah was five years older and the only one of the two who had kept a hint of their parents' northern accent.

Sarah leaned her head in further as if that would make him better understand her meaning. "As in false eyelashes. The ones I'm wearing have much more class." She turned her head to spy on her reflection over her brother's shoulder, her coiffed brunette hair pinned in place beneath a hot pink and orange feather fascinator. "Unlike Orla and her bridesmaids. They look like a bunch of knackers."

"I told you once and I'll tell you again," Jack began, pointing at her reflection in the mirror. "Our caravan is going to be the finest this side of the Shannon."

Sarah nearly snorted as she tried to stifle her laughter over the jest.

Jack's smile was crooked as he swept a hand through his brown hair that was too long and too unruly for his liking but, in contrast, was quite suited to Orla's liking.

"Da would be happy for you, Jack. So would mammy. She always wanted you to find yourself a nice girl. Whatever the fock that means."

He honed his attention on his sister, whose expression grew somber.

She cocked her head at him. "You probably barely remember Da."

"I was nearly six. I remember a lot."

"Mam was always afraid what you'd remember most about him was when she told you he'd been killed."

"Is Frankie here yet?"

Sarah nodded. "Snuck a kiss to my lips when I thought he was going for the cheek." She winced. "I t'ink I even felt his tongue."

"Belt him one for me."

"You know he isn't really an uncle."

"I used to picture Da fending off an army like Cú Chulainn," Jack said softly, his eyes somewhat unfocused.

"I t'ink the Troubles were all a bit less glamorous than that."

"What I remember most is his laugh and his rough hands... how he used to sing when I was meant to be sleeping, telling stories about growing up in Belfast and how families were thrown out of their homes during the Famine and how the *Púca* lived under the bridge in town."

Sarah laughed. "Used to scare me shiteless. I'd run across that bridge and never look over my shoulder every time I had to cross it." She glanced behind her as a guest pressed past her. She looked back at Jack. "They wanted this for you. For us. A peaceful life." She pursed her lips as she studied her brother's reflection. He wondered if she saw their father in the lines of his cheekbones and the shape of his eyes. "If only Da had also wanted that for himself."

Jack grunted in consent, adjusting his jacket in the mirror.

Sarah's face contorted into an ugly scowl. "Why *Orla*? You two have not'ing in common."

"Why does everyone keep saying that?" he asked as he twisted to look her in the eye.

"Even she's saying it."

"What do you mean 'she's saying it'?"

"I mean she's running around the place gushing 'what a catch, what a catch. He's a teacher, what a catch. We'll be hitched before my nan goes, t'anks be to God. Nan finally approved of a fella.'" Sarah fixed him with a deadpan expression.

"Her nan does love me."

"Her nan wants to ride you, and you know it."

A corner of Jack's upper lip lifted in a sneer.

"Christ's sake," Sarah continued, "she bought the girl her engagement ring."

"She only wants to see her granddaughter happy. Is that so terrible?"

Sarah twisted as someone muttered in her ear. She looked back at Jack. "The priest's got a bit of a tummy ache – he'll be out as soon as he can but it'll be a few minutes."

Jack nodded. His insides shuddered again. "I'm just gonna have a fag, so."

"So long as it's only a fag." She pointed at him, looking disturbingly like their mother. "No weed."

Sarah stepped out, closing the door behind her.

Jack puffed out his cheeks with an exhale, his brown eyes fixed on themselves in the mirror. He had lost most of his baby fat but strangers still routinely thought he was younger. His mouth curved slightly downwards at the corners and he often wondered if it was his unintentional pout that gave the impression of youth.

Thanks to Sarah, he now couldn't rid his head of the image of Orla's nan lounging on a bed, beckoning him hither in a negligee. His guts grated and he glanced at the time, wondering if he could take yet another shite before the ceremony started.

*How do I still have anyt'ing left to push out? It's nearly t'ree in the afternoon and I haven't eaten all day – how many days does it take for food to turn into shite? How long is that stuff sitting there? Maybe it's made on demand when the occasion called for it. Like now.*

Jack rummaged through the pockets of the trousers he'd worn to the church, fumbling for the last cigarette of the pack. He threw the clothing on the ground when he realized there was no lighter. Sticking the filter in his mouth, he stepped out of his changing room. Walking in a circle around the main chamber, he scanned the crowd for a familiar face but none were nearby.

*At my own fecking wedding.*

An array of tealight candles were alight on a table by the entranceway, next to a donations box with a sign that read, *Say a prayer for world peace*. Jack strolled over and held the end of his cigarette to one of the candle's flames then stuck it in his mouth. He crossed himself as he eyed the sign, remembering when it used to read, *Say a prayer for peace in Éire*.

He took a long drag, filling his lungs with the dark medicine.

Someone tapped his shoulder. "Jaysus fockin' Christ, this is a church. What're you t'inking, ya donkey's arse?"

Jack eyed the gray-haired man, finding relief in realizing that this fat fellow had no idea he was the groom.

"Out with the fag," the man spat, spittle spraying Jack's nose.

"Right. Sorry."

Jack sidled up to the nearest exit, stepping out into the damp air. A light mist fell but the sky over the Atlantic in the distance was clear. If not for the intermittent gales, it would be a beautiful Clare afternoon. A path wound away from the church and into one of the bordering farmer's fields, dotted with cattle and mottled with sunlight. The golden patches looked so inviting and made the green of the grass so vibrant that his feet were on the dirt before he registered what he was doing.

*Just a stroll to calm my nerves. Just until I'm done with the fag. Why didn't I t'ink to bring some weed?*

He glanced down to see how much smoke he had left and stepped in a cow patty.

"Oh, for fock's sake."

He hopped away, dragging the sole of his shoe across the wet grass. The ashes from his cigarette fell onto his jacket and he attempted dust them off only to have them smear a grey streak in the dampness. He rubbed but to no avail. Letting out a long exhale, he stamped out the rest of his cigarette and picked up the butt, glancing about for a rubbish bin. When he couldn't find one he stuffed it in his trouser pockets. Sweeping a hand through his unruly hair only made it catch the wind. Something about the tugging on his strands made him feel feverish and unsettled. Like a gale of wind himself. He was exhilarated and terrified and strangely horny.

*Jaysus, my head is up my arse.*

It was then that he began to reason that no sane man would get married in a stained suit with a soggy fag in his pocket to a woman who was putting the word "selfies" into her vows and filled the room with so many words that Jack scarcely had room to exhale his own.

A statue of the Virgin Mary faced him a few yards off behind the church, her cowled head bowed, her hands folded on one another. Her expression was serene as he approached, yet given the constant mist, a rivulet of water intermittently slipped past her eye and down her cheek. She was crying.

*Even the mother of Jaysus doesn't want me to get married.*

His heartbeat began to wrack his ribcage as he stood in place, his eyes locked onto the stone grey countenance of the Holy Virgin.

*Virgin?*

He hadn't minded so much that he'd let her down ages ago, with more women than he had fingers to count on, but now she was looking at him. Mary was watching. She'd always been watching.

*She fockin' knows Orla and I only met in that club because we each wanted to get the ride off the other. How did it escalate to this? Sex isn't love.*

One of the back doors of the church screeched as it opened and that was all the excuse Jack needed. He jumped and was off down the path, running like a rabbit. Running as if whoever was exiting the church was on his tail like a fox or a *Púca*. Angling into the field, he startled a few heifers who lowed and trotted away from him, their tails swishing. He ran and he ran and he didn't look back, twice slipping on the mud, his blood burning, thinking this would be easier if he didn't smoke so much. He heard his heartbeat in his ears, pounding like a drum, and he smiled, imagining his body was a jig, speeding over the green. As he crossed the brow of the hill and knew Mary couldn't see him anymore he felt weightless.

He felt free.

*Is this life? Will I always be running? What even is it that I'm running to?*

He didn't slow until he realized that his feet had taken him to Cliffs of Moher, nearly completely shrouded by mist. Ignoring the curious glances of the handful of backpackers as they passed by a man in a muddy, tailored suit on a walking path, Jack made his way to a viewing point. There he stood, catching his breath as the mist swirled around the headlands, forming a cloud. September days like this without much of a view usually thinned the tourists. He fell onto the seat of his trousers, ignoring the way the damp grass was already soaking into his boxers.

"The witch Mal fell madly in love with the hero Cú Chulainn," he muttered to himself. "When he refused her, she hunted him all over Éire until she finally caught up with him here. Cú Chulainn was still desperate to get away from her, so he leapt from the cliffs to the island of Diarmuid and Grainne's Rock." Jack paused and raised his brows, his breathing coming more steadily. The mist thickened upon the cliffs despite rising seven hundred feet out of the sea. "He could do that because he was the greatest Irish warrior that ever lived, but Mal... she was blinded by her desire. What do you t'ink she did, Jackie?"

Jack pursed his lips and shrugged, answering his father through himself. "I dunno, Da. Surely she didn't jump?"

"Ach, ay, she did," he continued in his father's Belfast lilt. "That she did, lad. And she fell right off the cliffs, staining the sea with her red blood."

*Oh, Da.*

The thought of his blood joining Mal's in the bay beneath him once Orla caught up with him made him laugh.

# 2

Five pints in and Jack was already thinking that the hairy mole on the middle-aged singer's face wasn't so bad after all, and the way she kept smiling at him... He stood up, his suit decorated with dried mud and smelling of a mixture of cow dung and cologne. He saluted her with his Guinness, the black stuff sloshing in the half-drunk glass as he climbed onto his chair. "Play us another one, love."

She laughed. "Sure, isn't that what I'm here for?"

His childhood friend Michael McGinty tugged on Jack's suit jacket, his eyes glinting in the yellowed lighting, combining with the tattoos on his neck to make him look fierce. "Sit *down*."

"Weren't they hired to play for me?" Jack slurred down at Michael.

"You're making an eejit of—"

"Look out, Mikey, I'm liable to piss on ya."

Michael scowled and leaned away as Jack feigned unzipping his fly. Jack laughed.

Several other pub-goers, who'd been let into McGann's once Jack told the barkeep that there wasn't going to be a private reception, after all, shouted for Jack to sit down. But the singer was still smiling at him.

"What'll it be?" she asked.

"A trad tune, to go with those blue, blue eyes of yours."

She grinned and winked then turned to her accompanying musicians who bore a guitar, accordion and *bodhrán* drum. They whispered for a few heartbeats while Jack hopped off the chair and slouched back into his seat, finishing his Guinness. While the white balloons and golden decorations hanging from the ceiling brightened the place up a bit, it was still dingy and for the first time, Jack understood why Orla had wanted the afters to be at a hotel.

The singer grabbed the mic as the drummer struck up a tune. "Alright, this one's for the would-be groom," she announced to a pub only half-interested while they gossiped about the wedding decorations. "What's your name?"

"Micky Collins."

"Right then – this one's for Michael Collins, the man himself!"

Jack laughed and clapped.

*I'm fockin' hilarious.*

He noticed his inked friend's less than amused expression. "What?"

Jack's new admirer began to sing.

*I wish I was in Carrickfergus*
*Only for nights in Ballygran*
*I would swim over the deepest ocean*
*Only for nights in Ballygran...*

Michael was shaking his head. "Haven't you caused enough trouble today?"

"I tell ya what, Mikey, even the Virgin Mary didn't want me nailed down. You shoulda seen it. Big tears running down her face."

*Oh but the sea is wide and I cannot swim over*
*And nor have I the wings to fly*
*I wish I could find me a handsome boatman*
*To ferry me over to my love and die*

"There were big tears running down Orla's face, too. I can't believe you'd do that to her."

"She's just embarrassed because all of Doolin was there to see her stood up."

*My childhood days bring back sad reflections*
*Of happy times I spent so long ago*
*My boyhood friends and my own relations*
*Have all passed on now like the melting snow*

Michael had a line between his brows. "Look at you. Talking like you're better than everyone else."

*But I'll spend my days in endless roaming*
*Soft is the grass I'm sure my bed is free*
*Oh, to be back now in Carrickfergus*
*On that long road down to the sea...*

"I am better than all those feckin' – fockin' – feckin'... did you know I didn't recognize a single one of 'em? Bunch of spineless spuds..."

Michael shook his head again. "The only spineless spud here is you. What is it that you're so angry at? And if you didn't want to marry the girl, then the least you could have done is told her before today."

Jack started laughing but the effort was forceful.

"Do you really t'ink I even knew before today?" Jack asked, his voice squeaking a small bit.

Michael sighed and studied the foam clinging to the side of his glass. "I don't see how you couldn't." He took a swig. "She's a nice girl."

"We would have made each other miserable. We didn't get along anywhere other than in the bedroom. In fact, she asked if I wanted to get married while we were in the middle of fockin'. I plea temporary insanity."

"Just shut up, Jack, you're drunk."

"She's dead!"

He turned around at the screech, facing his former fiancée. At least, he thought it was Orla, though he had never seen her so orange. "Oh, Christ."

She was wearing jeans and a sweater but her hair was still done up elegantly for the ceremony and her lips were a shade of pale pink that didn't make her look at all healthy.

"Jaysus, love, those are meant to be eyelashes, not a second pair of eyebrows."

She kicked one of the legs of his chair. "In the pew. She died in the pew while waiting for you to come out. No one knows when exactly. Hopefully, it was before she realized you weren't coming at all." Her fine features screwed up with wrinkles that stayed as her liquid foundation cracked.

"She was so full of wisdom," Michael commiserated. "'Nail that fine piece of arse down,' she used to say. God rest her soul. And she being all of fifty-eight."

"Eighty-five," Orla corrected.

"Just a kid," Michael sighed then stared into his pint.

"You're a right bollocks, Jack," Orla spat. "A thick, stunted, twisted piece of pasta mashed onto the bottom of my shoe that I've been walking on so long that it turned hard and black. That's what you are, you dirty bastard."

Jack leaned on the table as he climbed to his feet, facing her. "You sound so... convinced."

"I had all my friends there, two of my exes, and even got a Brazilian for tonight."

Jack's lower lip hung open as he studied her, holding onto the back of the chair, blinking as her perfume stung his eyes. "Look, I'm sorry about your nan. I'll forever miss the way she liked to pinch my bum. But I really don't see why you invited a South American to our honeymoon."

She shook her head. "You and your stupid pretty eyes."

"Listen, Orla," Jack slurred.

Her face turned a blotchy red. "This was supposed to be my day. *My* day! I was finally going to be the one in the dress, you commitmentphobe. I was finally going to be the envy of all my cousins and friends. The one with the perfect life and the hot husband. Taller than both of my exes. I had twenty-five people watching the livestream on my social media. *Twenty-five!*"

"Jaysus," Michael groaned, trying to hide his exasperation by taking another swig. "Livestreaming a wedding."

"Hey," Jack cautioned his friend with a finger. "Watch it now, she's a nice girl."

Orla stepped in-between them. "Do you have any idea how much my shoes cost?"

Jack couldn't look away from her heels. "They look painful alright."

"They will be when I turn you black and blue with them."

Jack swung his head towards Michael. "*Now* do you believe me?"

Orla brought her face up to Jack's. "If I never see you again it'll be too soon." She studied him with her mouth wrenched into a scowl, her eyes shimmering. "You're just a fockin' drunk."

She swallowed hard, giving him a few heartbeats to retort. When he only attempted to straighten his fecal-stained suit jacket she let out an incredulous gasp and shook her head before turning around and shoving past the other patrons to the exit.

Jack watched her weave through the bodies, his brow furrowing. "...Hey."

"Fock's sake, Jack," Michael mumbled as he rubbed his face. "I don't even know if *I* can stand being around you right now."

Jack was watching Orla exit the pub then looked back at Michael. "She left."

"Jaysus."

Jack slumped back into his chair. "Ya t'ink she's coming back?"

"I wouldn't."

"Piss off, Michael. Maybe I should go after her."

"It's over, Jack."

"Yeah? We can't just... go back to dating?"

Jack looked back to the exit, the last few minutes of his life churning in his mind as he realized the band hadn't finished the song and his parents were dead and Sarah had kids of her own so she was never around and that his attempt at broadening his family had just failed miserably.

*How am I supposed to know what to do?*

The musicians were all chatting and drinking. He stood up and wove his way over to them, smiling at the singer, his brown eyes seemingly focused on someone else just beside her.

"Hey, love." He gently grabbed the mic off the stand. "Give us a Republican tune."

The singer's smile faded as Jack grabbed the mic and it whined, irritating half the pub and making them go quiet. "Like what?"

"Like '*Tiocfaidh ár lá*,'" Jack slurred into the mic before it screeched terribly. Several patrons shouted at him to shut up and booed as the phrase "chuckie ar la" was announced over the speakers.

The singer wrenched the mic from his hand.

"You've had enough. Go on home now before you start trouble."

With that, she turned her back on him and switched off the mic.

Michael had nearly buried his face in one of his large hands. Jack didn't care that he was embarrassing his friend. Every once in a while he felt like he was floating, and it didn't have much to do with the alcohol. Instead, it had something to do with what was missing. With what was making his world feel so wrong.

It was in this dreamlike state that he saw Frankie enter McGann's.

The older man had a ruddy complexion and had a bigger belly than Jack remembered, but he would recognize his father's friend anywhere. Frankie didn't seem to take any notice of him standing by the band and instead batted away a balloon and made his way to the bar.

"And what's so terrible about starting trouble?" Jack belatedly asked the singer.

She hesitated before twisting her neck to look at him as if hoping that he was speaking to someone else.

"You've said your piece," the accordion player warned. "Now move on."

"I haven't said anyt'ing yet," Jack insisted. "Besides, this is my wedding day."

"You're not in Belfast," the singer snipped. "And you're hardly a big man. You're not'ing but an angry whippersnapper. You have no concept of what you're talking about."

"My da was a provo," Jack snapped. "So don't tell me that I don't know what I'm talking about, you stupid—"

Someone pegged him with a coaster. The cardboard Carlsberg ad hit him right in the temple, stirring a primal scream that silently burst in his chest. Jack spun around to face his casual assailant. A fat man shook his head at him from a barstool.

"Fock off, ya bastard," the fat man snapped. "Leave her be."

Jack only hesitated long enough to move into an attack position before tackling the fat man off his barstool.

"Oh, Christ," Michael groaned, hopping out of his chair and backing up as the stool skidded towards him. Shouts erupted in the pub, half of them asking the men to stop and the other half encouraging them to keep fighting. Jack and the other man tugged at each other's jackets and flailed about.

"He's a maniac," the fat man shouted. "A maniac!"

Jack was doing more grabbing than hitting as the other man struggled to get away from him.

*Why is everyt'ing spinning?*

"Hey!" The barkeep yelled, picking up a phone.

Michael kicked the stool away and slapped Jack's hands, prying him off the other man. "Get a hold of yourself!"

The other man staggered to his feet, poking at his large belly. "He pinched me!"

"I oughta bite you, you squaddie-loving fecker!"

Michael muttered an apology for his friend and shoved Jack towards the door.

"Fock's sake."

Jack nearly lost his footing several times as Michael hauled him as far away from the lights of the pub as possible. Once Jack realized that he was being manhandled, he squirmed free. Michael's foot slipped on the wet pavement and he had to splay his arms to catch himself. Jack stalked away.

"Where're you going?" Michael asked.

"Orla's."

"Like hell you are." He grabbed him by the arm.

Jack tried to yank his arm away but pulled too hard, losing his balance and falling over. He caught himself before he hit the ground then held still for a moment before his stomach lurched and he vomited foaming beer.

Michael winced and looked away. "Look at the cut of ya."

"I fockin' hate Oliver Cromwell," Jack coughed.

"You weren't alive then. None of us were."

"He was a fockin' fecker. I hate feckers."

"Christ, get over yourself, Jack."

Jack groaned and shifted to sit down, the cold of the pavement seeping into his pants. It reminded him of being by the Cliffs that afternoon and how beautiful they looked, even shrouded in mist. Everything seemed simpler then. He wished he could go back in time.

"Fock the English. And that focker inside..." He vaguely gestured to the pub. "...That place."

Michael studied him for a long moment, his nostrils flaring, then grabbed him by the jacket, hoisting him to his feet and slamming him against the side of the post office. "You're full of shite, Jack. You're twenty-five and a substitute teacher with no college education. Fock your da – you were never in the IRA – they were just a bunch of crack-dealers before the ceasefire anyway. They didn't give a shite about Ireland anymore. It's over. And you're just a fockin' parrot. The dole is giving you a chance at a good life. Make somet'ing of yourself, for Christ's sake."

Jack was glaring and tried to shove Michael away but the sober man just pressed harder against his shoulders. Jack's voice was weak. "Fock off."

Michael studied him for a long moment then let go, taking a step away. "T'ank God you didn't marry Orla. Imagine waking up to *you* every morning."

Jack wiped at a drab of spittle on his chin. "Imagine it?" he asked with a hoarse laugh. "I *do* it."

Michael shook his head. "Have a nice life. After you drink yourself to death, say hi to Pearse and Dev for me." He began to walk away then stopped to look at Jack and mockingly threw out his arms. "*Éireann go Brách!*"

Jack flipped him off. "Up your fockin' arse."

Michael kept walking.

"Right next to the queen's dick!"

Michael didn't look back. Jack chuckled to himself then became puzzled over the imagery of his own statement and sat down, his head swirling. He leaned against the side of the post office, rubbing his face, waiting for the world to stop spinning. It began to rain and he sat down and watched the drops pitter patter into his runny vomit, wondering how long it would take to wash away.

*Jaysus, was I really at the church just this morning?*

He shivered, hugging his knees to his chest. Michael was right. He was a fock up and the stench of stale beer on him was the mildest odor. Orla would never give him a second chance and he didn't want her to. She wasn't love; she was convenience and a warm body. His dead father would laugh and tell him he was better off a free man without a wife while his dead mother would be rolling over in the grave to fart in his direction.

"Jackie," a soft, deep voice said.

Jack looked up but in the near dark away from any building lights, he couldn't make out who was standing and staring at him in the rain.

*Da?*

Then the man lit a cigarette, and in the glow from his lighter, Jack recognized the light orange beard trying to hide the pockmarks of the man's skin. Frankie.

# 3

*By all accounts, Flint O'Connor was a jovial man. He shot from the hip and had a temper that you didn't want to ignite, but he could also be the most generous and welcoming of souls. Though madly in love with his wife, he paid no heed to the warnings of living a hard life of smoking and drinking and fighting.*

*At least, that's how people talk about him now. It's hard to ever know the truth about a matter when you're a generation removed and your most recent memories of a man are nearly twenty years old. It's funny how death seems to render us all into caricatures: the memories of the living produce accentuated versions of who we were in life once we're gone. So much so that the complications of a man fade and he is either one t'ing or the other.*

---

Jack had been on the train for hours that felt like days to his cramping muscles, watching the rainy countryside pass from Doolin to Galway, Westmeath to Kildare, Kildare to Dublin. Dublin – the city of the Black Lake. The economic heart of Ireland, it had been ground zero for the Viking and subsequent English invasions. The River Liffey divided the population by the haves and have nots. In recent years, the distribution of wealth had seen the divide between the impoverished and the well to do exacerbated at an alarming rate. It was a place that had seen many triumphs and atrocities.

*And it's about to get a fair sight better.*

Jack got off at Trinity College and paused to look around, taking a moment to light a cigarette and adjust to the perpetual motion of vehicles and people surrounding him. To his left was Grafton Street bustling with bag-toting tourists shopping and stepping over the pallid panhandlers bundled in blankets. Chinese and Eastern European immigrants hurried to work with earbuds connected to their skulls. Yanks and Australian tourists clustered around the tourist information building directly across from him. He would have to dodge to weave past all the rolling suitcases.

*No sign of any Dubliners in Dublin.*

He crossed the street and stuffed his cigarette into an ashtray on the side of a building, next to a picture of black lungs, then headed up the road, glancing at the hour. He still had time to wander about a bit before meeting Frankie for his ride to Finglas, just north of the city center.

Jack paused when he noticed words scribbled on a wall in black ink: *Provos = dead. New breed alive. Brits out.*

*What Brits?*

The only ones he could see were pensioners and students. He shook his head at the sloppy Sharpie scrawl.

*It's people like you yous that give us a bad name.*

As he spotted Dublin Castle in the distance, his disapproval extended to the riot that had erupted a decade or so past where shop windows were broken, cars were overturned and burned, and protestors chased the gardaí, or so he'd heard.

*It took a Unionist demonstration to lure the Dubliners into their own city.*

Young as he was at the time, half of him had wished that he'd been there to add to the madness — to chuck a petrol bomb at the bank — but the other half of him despised the rabble-rousers who only joined the fray after getting texts from their friends then headed off to drink imported lager after the riot.

*Weekend patriots.*

"Hey, excuse me."

Jack turned around to face a young homeless man, his coat tattered and his hair dreading.

"Do you have any change?"

"Sorry, boy."

The homeless man merely nibbled his dirty thumbnail in response. The weathering of his face made him appear older than his years, but Jack guessed that he was likely younger than him.

*Christ, look at the state of him. What will he do in the winter? At least he has a coat.*

The young man studied him for a moment then straightened, pulling his thumb away from his mouth. "To be honest, I'm gonna use it for cocaine. I have schizophrenia and it's the only t'ing that really helps."

"Good luck."

The two parted with curt nods. Jack sucked in a deep breath as a double-decker bus offering a city tour hauled past, much closer to the footpath than any bus would be back home. Everything about Dublin felt closer as if the city itself was determined to pick at his seams, invading his senses until it found its way in.

He knew that Belfast wasn't much different.

*How did you do it all those years, Da?*

---

Jack forced himself not to look out the window again as another large truck's breaks squealed just outside of the pub. Frankie picked over his fish and chips, pulling aside the breading.

"There's hardly any fish."

"What's wrong with the crispy bit?"

"Trying to watch my cholesterol," Frankie replied before he took the last bite of hake.

Jack started to smile, waiting for Frankie to laugh, but the ginger man simply fixed him with a patronizing stare, his pale blue eyes boring into Jack's from behind a pair of glasses.

"If you're lucky, one day, you'll be old, too."

Jack did let out a chuckle then before he took a swig of his red ale. "You've always looked the same to me. I swear you even had the beard when you came home with Da on my birthday when I was four or five and gave me a Kinder egg."

Frankie chuckled. "Christ, I barely remember that."

"My mam tried to take it away because she was worried I'd choke on the toy inside."

Frankie leaned back against his chair, a wistful smile on his face. "And what was the toy?"

"A miniature slinky."

The Belfast man shook his head. "You do have a good memory."

A server arrived to clear away their plates. They each placed an order for another drink then silence settled over the two. While Frankie didn't seem to take much notice and fixed his attention to the musicians setting up in the corner, Jack found himself fidgeting.

"So what's the story with Roscommon?" he asked softly.

Frankie merely raised a brow then darted his eyes towards the band.

*The fock?*

"I'm sorry I didn't make it to your mam's funeral," Frankie redirected. "It all happened so suddenly."

Jack nodded. "The doctors thought she had a good chance after the surgery. The infection set in very quickly, though. She hardly suffered."

"She was a good woman, your mam. And she was right to bring you lot out to Clare where trouble couldn't find you after your father died. T'ings were very tumultuous for a time."

The musicians started up "Whiskey in the Jar" and Jack winced at how loud their amps made the instruments. Anyone seated nearby could hardly hear the other.

"Aye, I was there at Roscommon," Frankie said, leaning in.

"Good man."

Frankie tapped his pink, pock-marked nose. "They had it coming and they know it."

The server set down their drinks then headed off to attempt to take orders at the next table amongst the din of the music.

"Makes me sick," Jack commiserated. "Throwing elderly people out of their homes just before Christmas?"

"Hey, watch it now, lad. I'm nearly elderly myself by that definition."

Jack smirked as he finished off his first pint then reached for his second.

"Eviction is always a dirty business," Frankie continued. "But to hire Brits to do a Euro bank's work in Ireland, to have the guards standing by, not intervening? Watching as their own people are dragged from their homes and left on the side of the road? And for what? Loans recalled by banks that were bailed out by the Irish taxpayer back in the recession?"

Jack nodded, focusing on Frankie's lips as well as his voice to not miss a word of what he was saying. "I'd say the banks don't give a fock."

"We're looking at fifteen-t'ousand evictions coming up. That's easily ten to thirty-t'ousand of our people homeless. May as well be the Famine."

*Just like Da used to say. Doors and windows being boarded up and all. Christ.*

"KCB Bank left private security in the house after the eviction. Over t'irty of us showed up and gave them a good hiding. Torched all their vehicles. I tell you what, the *craic* was mighty. Very satisfying."

Jack pursed his lips. "And the dog?"

"Christ, more people care about the fockin' dog than they do about the people."

"You have to admit, the dog dying is terrible PR."

Frankie gazed at him with unflinching pale orbs. "I'll be sure to relay your feedback to Human Resources for future retaliation raids."

"The dog was only doing his job."

"So were the security."

"But they were men. They made a choice. The dog couldn't."

"Look." Frankie continued, splaying his hand on the table, "we didn't mean to kill the fockin' dog. If they put it down, then that's their problem, not ours. It was about sending a message. Understand?"

Jack nibbled on a corner of his lower lip then leaned in closer, his voice as low as he dared. "So, what? We attack a bank? The security teams doing the evicting?"

Frankie shook his head, his glasses catching the light of a passing car outside. "We got our point across. They know we're still here. We'll be focusing on targets that are less... grandiose but still a part of the same problem. It's time to send a message to the dealers like they did in Tallaght."

A line formed between Jack's brows. "Dealers?"

"They're every bit as responsible for bringing death, corruption, and violence into our communities as the Brits were of old."

Jack shook his head. "But that's involving gangs—"

"Sure, what do you t'ink we are, lad?" Frankie asked, raising his fair brows. His pale eyes blazed with an intensity that Jack had only ever seen before in one of his ex's when she'd talk about *The Vagina Monologues*. "Some who have borne our name, who have called themselves the Irish Republican Army have defended these criminals, have even become dealers themselves. It's shameful. But they weren't the Real IRA. Sinn Féin is doing their part. With Brexit, we have more of an opportunity than ever before to bring Ulster back and finally be a united t'ity-two Counties. But if we're to free Ireland, we've got to free ourselves and our communities first."

Jack nodded, taking a sip of his red ale.

*Freedom.*

"If you weren't Flint's boy, I wouldn't be asking," Frankie continued. "I'll be there with you every step of the way. Now, do you t'ink you're up to the task?"

A series of memories flashed past in Jack's mind. Frankie giving him the chocolate egg. His father pinning the tricolors to the sitting room wall. His mother reminding him to not answer any questions about his father that were asked on the phone or by strangers. He took a deep breath then plastered on a smirk before mimicking Frankie's Belfast lilt.

"Ach, Ay."

Frankie slowly leaned back in his chair as he let out a long, low chuckle and threw Jack a wink.

# 4

*It's a strange t'ing, losing your father before you've properly started school. Sarah always says that mam was never the same after Da died. That she aged quickly and spent more and more time in bed. I have to take her word for it because I don't remember my mam behaving any differently than that. I don't remember a time when Sarah wasn't doing most of the cooking and getting me up for school on time.*

*What I do remember is the first time I felt that rage. Tommy Malone's mother was from Bristol and he liked to boast about their football team. One day, he took it too far and said they'd slaughter any one of our teams any day, same as my da was killed by an Englishman. Needless to say, my bruised fists and I were suspended. Tommy grew up and moved away.*

*I never stopped feeling the rage after that day.*

*God help me.*

Jack peered out the back window of the parked car, ignoring the nuisance of the tightly-collared military jacket against his throat, watching the guard station along with Frankie and another fellow close to the ginger's age named Stephen who had less of a gut than Frankie but also less hair.

It was night and they'd been parked on the corner for several minutes and while they were supposed to be watching for signs of movement inside, it was hard for Jack to not let his mind wander. He kept thinking of the old people left on the side of the road after being dragged out of their homes in Roscommon, and the looks on Michael and Orla's faces that night at McGann's after he stood her up.

Something about what he was doing now made it all feel justified. He wasn't sure what law he had broken, but he knew he had broken one by calling in a bomb threat to the guard station he was staring at now. Never mind that he had never even seen a bomb in his life, much less a gun until two days ago when Frankie gave him a rifle along with a brief lesson on how to use it that didn't include any actual shooting. The weight of the weapon on his lap and the way Frankie's Belfast tones had blended with his father's voice in his head made him feel removed from Clare entirely. Far from any disappointment.

His lawlessness was a shield against their expectations.

*Not because I'm making somet'ing of myself... more like because I'm unmaking somet'ing of myself. You can't place any expectations on not'ing.*

"Right. They've all fecked off. The bomb squad will be here soon," Frankie muttered as he started the engine.

Jack bit the corner of his lower lip, flushed with adrenaline as the lights from the city glossed over the windshield.

Stephen looked at him through the rearview mirror. "You all right, O'Connor?"

Jack offered the elder man a curt nod.

"Your family is like mine. Long history of Republicanism."

"Yeah?" He hesitated, shaking one leg for a moment. "And did my da ever talk about me?"

Stephen chuckled as Frankie muttered a curse when he was forced to enter a line of traffic. "Wouldn't shut up," Stephen replied. "I didn't have kids then, so I didn't understand. Now I do."

"They say it changes you, all right," Jack offered.

Stephen nodded. "The responsibility. Your life is no longer your own — it belongs to them, as well."

"Fock's sake," Frankie muttered, even as the traffic eased up and they were driving again.

"I'll be running from that myself for some time yet," Jack replied, thickening his Clare accent, making the two other men chuckle.

Stephen turned on the radio, skimming over the airwaves, pausing once for the weather report and to hear how the Dublin boys in blue, or Gaelic Football team, were faring, then settled on Kesha's pop song, "Die Young."

Before long, all three were bobbing their heads in time with the upbeat tune. Stephen started singing along under his breath. Though the song was hardly new, Jack was still impressed by how many lyrics the balding man knew. He was about to ask if Stephen had a teenaged daughter when Frankie parked the car outside of a large building complex.

"This is it," Frankie muttered.

Jack peered out at what he could see of the structure. The modern style felt out of place among the city's famous Georgian architecture.

He expected there to be a question to ask if he were ready or another rundown of the plan. Instead, Frankie killed the engine and Kesha's song with it, leaving Stephen's voice the only one continuing the hit. He silenced himself the moment Frankie donned his balaclava. The ginger man hopped out of the vehicle, leaving Jack bathed in a flush of heat as he scrambled to ready himself, awkward in his gloves. He yanked his own balaclava over his face but had to tug at the eyeholes to adjust it, a tuft of brown hair sticking out of one.

Frankie and Stephen had theirs on prim and proper in just one go.

*Like women shouldering their purses.*

He shoved the hair back in then pulled his rifle out from under the seat. The older two were ready and waiting. Frankie merely glanced to ensure that Jack was ready then hurried away from the vehicle.

As he followed, Jack noticed each streetlamp and glowing window with the raising of a new hair on the back of his neck. Though completely covered, he had never before felt as if he had such a soft, exposed belly, or a name tag printed on both his front and his back. His face burned.

The lobby was empty when they entered. Jack turned towards the stairwell then paused when the other two walked past him towards the lift.

Jack kept his head bowed, the burning in his face spreading throughout his body as he wondered how many cameras were filming him right now as he walked back over to the two.

The lift hummed in the quiet but didn't arrive.

Stephen cleared his throat. "You did push it?"

"See, the button's glowing there," Frankie softly replied, picking at a black tuft of lint on his military jacket. "Meant to grab my other balaclava. This one pills terribly. I've fluff all over." He brushed at his chest.

With a chime, the lift arrived and opened. Jack stepped in with the other two, relieved that it was vacant.

"The fock aren't we taking the stairs?" he asked once the doors were closed, bending his knees and flexing his hands around the stock of his rifle to try to burn off some of his energy. "I thought that was the plan."

Stephen jerked his head towards Frankie. "It was 'till his knee gave out in the run through yesterday."

"His knee?" Jack repeated.

"I told ya, Jackie," Frankie warned, "it doesn't pay to get old."

"The right one, is it?" Stephen asked.

"Left. I had the right replaced, oh, about t'ree years ago now."

"Right, right. And is the left any better today?"

"It is," Frankie replied.

"One can never be too careful though."

"Ach, ay. I'll be gentle for a few days yet."

The lift chimed and opened its doors.

"You're sure this is the right floor?" Stephen softly asked.

Frankie nodded then burst out of the lift, startling Jack so much that he fell back and let the two elder men take the lead. Rifles at the ready, they scurried down the hallway, Frankie all the while muttering, "Sixteen, sixteen, sixteen..."

Jack trotted behind the two. A TV was loudly heard as the door in front of them to the right opened. Frankie and Stephen lowered their guns and stopped so suddenly that Jack walked right into Stephen's back.

A thirty-something woman in loungewear, her bleached hair tied up in a messy bun, was fishing her keys out of her purse as she closed the door to her flat.

*Fock.*

She did a double-take when she noticed them just a few feet from her, her brown eyes widening and her mouth forming a thin line. She made no move to go back inside and the men in balaclavas all stared at her for several seconds. Then Frankie cleared his throat softly and stepped aside, making way. Stephen mimicked him, punching Jack in the arm when he didn't budge. The Clare man hopped out of the woman's path.

"Evening," Stephen greeted.

She stiffly started past them, still staring. "Evening."

"Where you off to then, love?" Frankie asked.

"Milk for tea."

"Do us a favor and buy local," Stephen advised, prompting her to halt. "It's the small co-ops that are struggling these days."

"I thought dairy was subsidized by the EU and that it was the beef farmers who were struggling," she offered in a rush.

Jack nodded. "I heard that, too."

The woman's eyes darted to him, her spine rigid.

"Just goes to show, you can't trust everyt'ing you read on Facebook," Stephen lamented. "In that case, just avoid the stuff with antibiotics and RBST."

She nodded. "I always do." The woman began her stiff walk down the hall again.

"Oh, and love?" Frankie asked, jerking his head towards her purse. "No mobiles."

"Jaysus," she gasped. "When did Dublin become Derry?"

Frankie raised his rifle. "Just keep walking."

"There's no need for that," Stephen snipped while the woman power-walked towards the lift.

"She's seen us," Jack whisper-gasped. "She'll call the guards."

"Who are busy with their bomb scare, now Christ's sake," Frankie hissed as he resumed his trot down the hallway. Jack thought he caught the movement of a door being cracked open out of the corner of his eye but didn't dare say anything lest he anger Frankie further.

The Belfast man paused outside of flat sixteen within seconds. The other two fell into position by flanking him, pointing their rifles at the ceiling. With a nod, Frankie rapped on the door. No one answered. He knocked again.

"Yeah?" a male voice answered.

"Domino's delivery," Stephen announced.

"Wrong flat," the voice from inside replied, sounding distracted.

"This is for..." Stephen paused to feign reading, "Ryan Walsh."

"Babe?" the man inside called.

Footsteps shuffled. A woman with wet, combed hair draped over the shoulders of her pink robe unlocked the door. As soon as it was open an inch, Frankie kicked it. The woman let out a gasp as the door struck her in the face. She stumbled backward and Jack followed the two men inside then slammed it shut behind him.

The only thought Jack had was how odd it was that he couldn't think. He could take in the newness of the flat, the widescreen TV and the way Ryan Walsh fumbled with his game controller at the ruckus, sending his digital vehicle crashing. He could hear a toddler's voice asking for his mammy from the room opposite the entryway, and smelled fruity shampoo wafting out of the bathroom on the hot, moist air. But he couldn't account for the way his arms held the rifle aimed at Ryan or why the woman with the bloody nose's cry to please not hurt them sounded like something coming from the television and not the human being holding her arms out for her three-year-old son who sleepily exited the bedroom.

"Christ, take whatever you want," Ryan insisted, his hands held up. He was in a pair of black trackies and a navy blue hoodie. Though he lacked the ink, his piercings and size reminded Jack of Michael.

"We aren't here to rob you, you dirty bastard," Frankie barked. "Have you any idea who we are?"

"Domino's collection agency?" Ryan asked.

Frankie took a step towards him, the rifle aimed between the dealer's eyes. "You t'ink you're funny, do ya?"

"Christ's sake," Ryan barked, "just tell me who yous work for."

"Please," Ryan's wife begged as she picked up their son. "*Please.*"

Jack had his rifle trained on Ryan but swung it around to the woman when she spoke. Pressing the child to her chest, she squeezed her eyes shut. The gears of his mind started to churn again and he realized she was afraid of him. He shifted his rifle so that it was aimed just off to her side. Her watery hazel eyes met his brown, the joints in her hands white as she clung to her son's pajamas. The small trickle of blood stemming from her nose seemed to have stopped. The boy peered curiously at the masked men, one side of his face stamped with the pattern of his blankets, still looking half asleep. Then he let out a soft "ow," and twisted a little, peering up at his mother's face.

*She's holding him too tightly.*

"Who we work for?" Stephen repeated with a hoarse chuckle. "That would be *Plobacht Na hÉireann.*"

"How dare you bring such corruption into our country," Frankie announced, making his voice deeper than normal and locking eyes with the dealer. "You should be ashamed of yourself. Poisoning your fellow Irish."

"No one forces them to buy," Ryan evenly retorted.

Frankie closed the distance between them and pressed the barrel of his rifle against Ryan's belly. The younger man fought to hide the quaking of his jaw. "You've t'ree days. If you don't clear out by then, we kill you."

Jack watched as the child squirmed again but his mother's hands still looked like talons.

*Too tightly...*

Frankie's voice was a growl. "Understood?"

Ryan nodded several times.

"You're lucky we're not killing you right now," Stephen added.

Frankie and Stephen started backing towards the door. Jack mimicked them and thought he saw the woman's lips mouth the words "thank you."

Stephen hit Jack's arm to redirect his attention. The younger man slipped out into the hall. It was clear. He swallowed but his mouth was dry.

*I haven't had weed in ages. Why do I have cottonmouth?*

"T'ree days," Frankie repeated as he and Stephen backed out to join Jack.

Just then, the same door Jack had seen crack open earlier swung wide. Thirty-odd feet away, Jack only had time to make out the pumpkin-shaped, balding head of a man before an arm swung up, pointing a handgun at him. Jack's heart and lungs hitched. He squeezed his trigger, the kick of the rifle rattling his flighty frame, making him think he had been shot as it slammed into his shoulder. He cried out as his knees buckled and rammed against the floor. The impact made him squeeze the trigger again and the window at the end of the hall shattered. He had missed his target.

*T'ank God.*

The briefest flashes of fire erupted from the handgun as the baldy shot back. Frankie and Stephen were on either side of Jack, shouting and returning fire. It was loud. All too loud to think. The door to flat sixteen was slammed shut. The baldy's head snapped back with a black hole just above one of his eyes and he fell over dead.

# 5

Frankie yanked Jack up by the scruff then let go as they bolted for the stairwell. Jack couldn't catch up with what was happening. He was sure now that he had been smoking. Nothing felt real and the rifle in his hands was held so effortlessly. As if it were made of driftwood. As they rounded a corner on the stairwell, he stumbled into the other two.

Frankie roughly shoved him against the wall. "My fockin' knee!"

Once back out in the darkness, Jack noticed that the air felt odd. It wasn't until he was yanking open the car door that he realized it was drizzling. Tossing his rifle inside, he heard the driver's door slam shut. Frankie looked behind him as he started the engine, backing out before Stephen and Jack had even shut their doors. Jack was slammed back against the seat as the Belfast man hit the gas and they sped off.

"Jaysus." Jack yanked off his balaclava with quaking hands, his hair sticking up haphazardly. "Fock!" He grabbed his right shoulder to double-check that he hadn't been hit and that it was only throbbing from the kick of the rifle.

"You're all right, O'Connor," Stephen assured from the passenger's seat.

"Like hell, he is," Frankie growled then chanced a look at his comrade as he navigated the side streets. "And like hell, he doesn't know!"

"Christ, slow down, they've traffic cameras all over the place here."

"You're really worried about a speeding ticket?"

The flashing of the street lights as they zoomed beneath them reminded Jack of the sparks from the baldy firing and the soft little choking sound he had made as the bullet ground into his skull. Jack's stomach churned and his skin grew cold. He closed his eyes and concentrated on his breathing, fighting back nausea. The two in the front seats were yanking off their balaclavas as they quarreled. Though he tried, he couldn't hold onto their words long enough to even begin to understand what it was about.

The next thing he knew, Frankie was pulling over where there were no streetlights. Jack barely had time to peer around at the vacant lot surrounded by a chain-link fence before the Belfast man flung open his door. He yanked him out of the car, shoving Jack onto the wet ground.

"Fock, O'Connor!"

The chill in the air and the wet against his skin sharpened Jack's senses. He scrambled to his feet, spinning around to face Frankie. Frankie socked him in the face. Jack's teeth clanked together and a fireblossom of pain burned his cheek. He stumbled from the blow, holding a hand to his mouth as his cheek seemed to both swell and grow numb at the same time. Letting out a gasp, he watched the two over his shoulder, only able to see one half of each of them in the headlights. Frankie yanked a club out of the boot of the car.

"What the fock are yous doing?" Jack barked.

The Belfast man didn't reply as he advanced on Jack.

"That's enough, Frankie!" Stephen hissed.

Jack tried to run but Frankie hit him in the lower back, knocking him over. The younger man coughed out a cry and landed on his shoulder, giving it a real reason to ache.

"Trying to get me killed, were ya?"

Jack landed a rabbit kick to Frankie's bad knee.

The ginger howled and nearly lost his footing.

"Christ's sake," Stephen groaned as he stalked over to the two.

Sirens echoed in the distance as the guards belatedly responded to the emergency calls from Ryan's building and from several others throughout the section of the city where the RIRA had issued warnings to dealers.

Frankie screamed and slammed his baton against a nearby chain link fence.

Jack got to his feet, wiping away what he realized was blood from his split lip. "One of you shot him, not me."

Frankie faced him again with a howl and Jack ducked as the older man swung at his side and missed. Frankie recovered his momentum. He brought the club down again, connecting with Jack's ribs. Jack cried out but the blow was dampened by Stephen shoving Frankie away in mid-strike. "Jayus, he's one of us, Frankie!"

"Not anymore, he isn't," Frankie gasped. "He wants revenge." Frankie jerked away from Stephen.

"Damnit, Frankie, I told you — he *doesn't know!*"

"Like fockin' hell. He ducked right when that bastard fired. Made me a fockin' target. I heard one hit the wall right by my fockin' face!"

The older man's shouting was as loud as the cracking of the waves at the base of Moher.

*I want to go back to that place. I want to stretch towards the horizon.*

Jack couldn't focus on either of them as searing heat radiated from his bruised side. "She was holding him too tightly," he gasped.

Stephen grabbed Frankie by the collar, his voice gravelly and low. "If he'd wanted to kill you, he would've shot you already. He *doesn't* know. His mam never even knew."

Frankie took a moment to catch his breath. It clouded before him in the headlights, making him seem bigger than he was. He studied Jack who straightened, a hand pressed to his bruised side, glancing between the two.

"What didn't she know?" the Clare man croaked past the burning and pinching in his chest.

Frankie pulled away from Stephen, tucking the club under his arm. "You know how Flint died?"

Jack licked his lips, tasting copper, struggling to stay in the moment. Everything hurt and the headlights were so glaring and the only thing that felt real was the cold. The glorious, numbing cold.

"He was killed in Derry. By a squaddie."

Frankie shook his head, his voice quaking with his dissipating anger. "He and I were part of the provos."

"Christ, now's hardly the time, Frankie," Stephen barked.

Frankie swallowed, his shoulders rising and falling as he caught his breath. "Everyone thought the Troubles were coming to an end... there were five of us holed up in a building. The Brits had us surrounded and were picking us off with snipers. It had been t'ree days... no food, just rainwater... t'ree of our friends were shot and we had to watch them die. Hear their terror as they drew their last breaths and bled out. We sat there with their bodies, just waiting for our turn. There was gunfire every once in a while as the other provos tried to distract the bastards so we could escape."

"We even threw a pipe bomb at the fockers," Stephen added, a dark light dancing in his eyes as he pulled his military coat collar closer around his neck.

"We didn't find out 'till afterward, but the Brits thought Gary Adams was in there with us — he was in our Army Council. Huge warrant for him. And the way our lads were fighting to distract them, you'd believe it."

Jack wrapped his arms around himself with a small shiver. The cold was now easing his bruises. Or maybe it was something else. Maybe it was knowing that a greater pain was about to come.

Stephen glanced at the distant street. "We should clear out, lads."

"Few times a day they'd get on a speaker and say if we came out they wouldn't shoot," Frankie continued. "That they'd give a lighter sentence to anyone who'd give them information. On that t'ird day, the bodies were bloated and stinking, and your da kept talking about you and your sister..."

*Rough hands. Tales of the* Púca *under the bridge in Doolin. "Shh, keep this a secret so that Mammy doesn't know I kept you up."*

Jack let out a long breath, the air streaming before him in a white puff. He was standing at his full height. "He wanted to take the deal. And they shot him."

Frankie shook his head, half of his face haloed by the harsh headlights. "No, lad. It was me that shot him."

Jack's blood suddenly rushed past his ears like the sound of the surf back home.

*Am I the sea? But you gave me the Kinder egg.*

The Belfast man's voice was quiet. "He was gonna turn us all in."

Stephen began to pace. "We need to *go.*"

Jack stopped hugging himself and let his arms swing down to his sides, his biceps constricting with his fists. "Why the fock did you shoot him?"

"I tried to talk him out of it but he wouldn't listen. It was the only way."

"There," Stephen said to Frankie. "You see? He didn't know. He wasn't trying to get you or either of us killed. Let's *go.*"

He headed for the car.

"'The only way?' Christ, what's wrong with you?" Jack took a step towards Frankie, his brow furrowed in a frown. "You got out, didn't you? Why couldn't you just wait? Tie him up and fockin' *wait*?"

"You have no idea what it was like," Frankie growled, and the whites of his eyes glinted. "I thought there was no way out. I thought we'd all die but couldn't risk bringing everyone else down with us. Not for the sake of one man."

Jack took another step towards Frankie then paused when Frankie un-tucked the baton from under his arm. The younger man's eyes began to shimmer. "And what the fock was this? Redemption?"

Frankie kept his eyes on Jack's. "He was my friend, Jackie. A brother. Not a day goes by that I don't pray for forgiveness for what I did. If I could change it all, I would. But I can't."

Jack's bruised lip sneered as a pair of tears fell. "You're a murderer."

Frankie was quiet for a moment, watching as the moisture slipped down Jack's cheeks. "In the eye of the beholder. And don't t'ink the guards don't admire us for killing drug dealers." He paused to gauge Jack's response but the younger man merely blinked out more tears. "We're freeing Ireland, lad. We're heroes."

"You killed him just like you killed that man," Jack gestured vaguely towards the building.

"He would've killed *us*."

"He wasn't a soldier or a dealer!"

"And neither was your da but sometimes people have to die."

Jack's chest heaved past the pain in his ribs and he distantly registered the sound of Stephen starting the engine. Frankie glanced to the car as the headlights shifted then looked back at Jack. Jack rubbed the tears off his cheeks with a gloved palm sticky from being on the wet gravel.

Frankie eyed him a heartbeat longer. "We were kids then. Just fockin' kids." The Belfast man then turned his back on Jack, heading for the car.

Jack hesitated a moment then followed as if tethered to Frankie. His feet didn't feel like his own. Nor his hands that had held a rifle or the skin of his face that now stank of someone else's fabric softener. The only thing that felt like his own, the only thing he owned, was the pain.

He ducked into the car. Stephen was in the driver's seat and had the heater on full blast and it was fogging up the windows.

"Mam never knew?" Jack softly asked once Frankie was back in the vehicle.

"Only me and Stephen and two men who are now dead ever knew. Everyone else thinks it was a British bullet." He glanced at Jack but couldn't hold his gaze. "So what now? You going to put a bullet in *my* head?"

Jack pressed his swelling lips together, exhaling through his nose as he shook his head.

Frankie looked at him full on then. "Why not?"

"Because I'm not a murderer."

# 6

*Did you ever hold me that tightly, Da? Did you ever hug me until it hurt? Mam was never one for hugs, but I know that you were. And I know that you held me so tightly in your mind that it hurt. So tightly that you were willing to face the gunfire and the shame and the bullet that would inevitably find you for squealing. Squealing. You weren't just a man. You were all of us. You died for putting your family first. Putting love first.*

---

Three days later, Jack was back outside the complex in Finglas. Alone, he was wearing jeans and a dark blue jumper. After his outburst and beating, Frankie had reluctantly agreed to let Jack handle this his way. Besides, the ginger needed to ice his knee.

A guard was outside the building in his car, looking bored as he swiped on his phone. Some white roses grew off to the side. They had seen better days but Jack picked a handful anyway, which was easier said than done without pruners, then started towards the entrance.

Once in the stairwell, he reached into his coat and switched the safety off the pistol in his waistband. Up on the proper floor, Jack returned the smile of an older woman who passed by him, glancing at his roses with a twinkle in her eye. He offered her a wink then kept going.

*My split lip and bruises must be rather becoming. Or she has terrible cataracts.*

He passed by the flat where the pumpkin-headed man had lived. While Jack understood that he would never truly make peace with knowing he had a hand in the bystander's death, in the days following the man's murder, he had come to rationalize that no truly innocent man would have an unregistered firearm waiting at his disposal, to say nothing of randomly opening fire.

*Not that that makes it ok that he died by our hand.*

Jack reached flat sixteen.

Taking a moment to steel himself, Jack knocked. No one answered.

*T'ank Christ.*

He knocked again. The dealer's wife cracked open the door.

"Oh, for fock's sake," he muttered under his breath, lowering the roses in his hand.

She narrowed her eyes a little when she didn't recognize the young man. "Yes?"

"I have flowers for flat sixteen."

The woman opened the door a crack more. Jack had already stepped inside by the time she realized that the stems weren't wrapped in cellophane.

"Ryan!" she called.

"Really?" Jack asked. "The same fockin' ruse?"

Jack slammed the door shut and stood in front of it. Tossing the roses aside, he pulled out his gun and aimed it at the woman. Her nose was bruised but healing. The dealer stumbled into the room from the kitchen, wearing trackies and an undershirt. "Why the fock did you answer the door, Nancy?"

"Don't move!" Jack shouted, swinging the gun between the pair. "Keep your hands where I can see them."

Both held up their hands.

Jack chanced a quick look around. The flat was emptier than

before but still showed signs of being lived in — plates on the table, a computer left on, displaying an e-bay page. "Where's your son?"

"He's staying with his nan," Nancy responded.

Jack shook his head, his voice cracking as he pleaded. "Why in God's name didn't yous move out?"

"There was a murder here last week. There's a guard outside—" Ryan began.

"And a fine watch he's keeping, isn't he?" Jack adjusted his grip on the gun.

"I've seen your face," Ryan argued. "I can identify you."

"I'm here to kill you, you fockin' retard."

"I told you this would happen." Nancy was tearing up. "Why didn't you listen to me? Now he'll kill us both!"

"Yeah, why didn't you listen to her, Ryan?"

Ryan shook his head. "My mother-in-law hates me."

Jack raised his brows. "Sound woman."

"I have nowhere else to go."

"I'm sure the divil will make room for you."

He stepped forward and Nancy gasped as Jack pressed the barrel against Ryan's forehead. Ryan squeezed his eyes shut, muttering a prayer under his breath as his wife dropped to her knees and covered her ears, screwing her eyes shut. Jack dug the metal harder against the man's skull, leaning in until he was inches away from his head, then whispered, "Bang."

Jack pulled the gun away.

Ryan opened his eyes.

Nancy looked up.

Jack took a few steps back. "Get your gear. Get your lad's gear. You're leaving right now."

Nancy sagged then stumbled to her feet. "Oh t'ank you, t'ank you..."

"Don't t'ank me, just get the fock out. Now."

Ryan was still standing there in sweaty shock.

When he didn't show any signs of movement Jack took a step towards him and kicked him in the buttocks. "Now!"

Ryan recovered his senses and dashed down the hall after his wife.

Jack followed them, watching as they grabbed possessions. "Hurry up. The lads waiting for me in the van outside expect me to be shooting you." He knew that in their panic, the couple would never notice that there was no van.

"T'ank you so much for not killing me," Ryan simpered as he shoved his shaving supplies into his pillowcase. Jack studied him for a moment then faintly nodded.

Nancy grabbed her coat then looked at Jack. He hesitated as he remembered her grip on her boy. He couldn't meet her hazel eyes.

"Out the fire escape," he instructed. "And make one move towards that guard and I'll blow you to fock."

She nodded then opened the window, climbing out with her bag. Jack looked back at Ryan as he moved to exit with his wife then stopped, doubling back to get a teddy bear out of his wardrobe.

He glanced to Jack as he did so. "My son's. Declan can't sleep without it."

"Then why's it in your wardrobe?" Jack stepped over and snatched the bear from him, noticing a tear in the seam. He yanked at the fabric and packages of white powder fell out. Ryan locked eyes with Jack for several heartbeats.

Jack slammed him against the wall. "You fockin' chancer."

Water started trickling. Something was spilling nearby. Jack hastily glanced around in confusion. Then he smelled it. He looked down at his feet then back up at Ryan. The dealer had just weed his trousers.

---

On the train west, Jack leafed through the paper and had to look through it twice to find the article. He grinned, the Roscommon countryside sliding past outside the window beside him.

**DEALER CAUGHT WITH TEDDY BEAR**

DUBLIN – Local drug dealer Ryan Walsh was arrested in his flat in Finglas early Wednesday morning. Walsh, 36, had been bound to his bed with a teddy bear stuffed with cocaine. A note was pinned to his shirt that read: "I pissed my pants and I sell drugs." Garda Chief O'Malley says, "This was obviously orchestrated by an anti-drug vigilante group and I need to stress the importance of allowing the law to strictly deal with these matters." Reports of RIRA activity in the neighborhood were rumored but garda officials would not comment. It is suspected that the murder of Paul O'Brien the previous week is linked to the vigilantes. O'Brien was wanted by the garda for seven counts of human trafficking. No individual suspects have been identified.

"Poor bastard," Jack muttered, folding up the paper as the snack trolly started its rickety path down the car. There was a war in his mind between pity and guilt over the loss of life, and satisfaction that justice had been served, swiftly and painlessly... and completely by dumb luck.

Frankie had understood why Jack said that he needed to go home.

There was a stop up ahead. If he was quick he could step out long enough to have a few drags from a cigarette. As he rummaged through his coat pocket for his lighter, he felt something smooth and oblong. Pulling it out, he smirked at the white and orange foil.

*A fockin' Kinder egg.*

Looking out the window, he watched the bogs roll past with their heather-covered rises.

Soon he would pass the barrenness of the stony Burren.

"To hell or to Connacht," he whispered.

---

*There are many different kinds of love. So much is said about the passion between lovers who are just strangers, really, brought together by hormones and shared experiences. Then there are the tales about the bond between a parent and child.*

*Less often heard is the story of just how much a child can love their parent, even in their absence. Especially in their absence. So much so that it can lead a man astray. But it it isn't the missing or the hole left behind that guides the wayward son; it's the loving, the forever searching for a figure just beyond the Atlantic horizon, never comprehending what I was truly yearning for.*

# EPILOGUE

The Cliffs of Moher rose out of the sea like breaching, earthen monstrosities of the deep. Jack O'Connor stood upon their edge. He had scarcely been away from Doolin for a month and in that time, Michael and Orla had started dating after allegedly sharing a moment at her nan's funeral. Assuming the worst, Sarah had started planning her little brother's eulogy. She threatened to kill him all the same when he returned and told her the truth about what he had been up to in Dublin. She made him vow to never take part again. It was an easy enough promise to make. As was that to complete his History degree after Sarah and her husband offered to help pay his tuition.

The wind on the Cliffs was savage. It stung his skin and made his nose and eyes run while it whipped his brown locks across his forehead. But there was no mist today. The headlands made the waves cracking against their bases hundreds of feet below look like the tufts of dandelions blown by the breeze.

"Oh, Da," he whispered.

It was all he could say and all he needed to say. Because he understood now that Cú Chulainn was just a story. A metaphor. That Ireland had many warriors, and most of them had never even touched a weapon. And that the best way he could honor his father and truly find freedom was not with a gun.

*Because I know you're in me, Da. You've been inside me all along. The one place I never thought to look. The one place I'm forced into now. The piece of me I have never loved but am awakening to more and more every day.*

The sun was dazzling upon the sea. Jack smiled.

After all, what is the ocean but a mirror for the sky?

# THANK YOU FOR READING!

If you enjoyed this book, then please consider leaving a star review on your favorite platform.
   **Click here.**

# GLOSSARY OF IRISH TERMS

- *Craic* – Irish (Gaelic) for fun, good times, laughter, good conversation, entertainment, news.
- *Éirinn go Brách* – Irish (Gaelic) for "Ireland forever/Ireland until eternity." Allegiance to Ireland.
- **Feckin'** – A version of a rude word that is acceptable in polite society.
- **IRA** – Irish Republican Army.
- *Poblacht na hÉireann* – The Republic of Ireland.
- **Provo** – A member of the provisional Irish Republican Army.
- **Púca** – A mythological creature that could bring either good or bad luck and usually causes mischief.
- *Sinn Féin* – Left-wing, Irish Republican political party. Irish (Gaelic) for "we ourselves/ourselves."
- *Tiocfaidh ár lá* – Irish (Gaelic) for "our day will come," referring to a united Ireland.

# ABOUT THE AUTHOR

K.M. Rice is a national award-winning screenwriter and author who has worked for both Magic Leap and Weta Workshop.

Her four-part Afterworld series debuted with *Ophelia* and continues with *Priestess*.

Her first novel, *Darkling*, is a young adult dark fantasy that now has a companion novel titled *The Watcher*. Her novella *The Wild Frontier* is an ode to the American spirit of adventure and seeks to awaken the wildish nature in all of us. She also provided additional writing and research for *Middle-earth From Script to Screen: Building the World of The Lord of the Rings and The Hobbit*.

Over the years, her love of storytelling has led to producing and geeking out in various webshows and short films. When not writing, filming, or galavanting around Ireland, she can be found hiking in the woods, baking, running, and enjoying the company of the many animals on her family ranch in the Santa Cruz Mountains of California.

facebook.com/KMRiceAuthor
twitter.com/kmriceauthor
instagram.com/kmriceauthor

# ALSO BY K. M. RICE

### Dark Fantasy

- *Darkling*
- *The Watcher (A Companion Novel to Darkling)*

### Historical Fantasy

- *Ophelia (Afterworld Book One)*

### Historical Fiction

- *The Wild Frontier*

### Other

- *Middle-earth From Script to Screen: Building the World of the Lord of the Rings and The Hobbit*
- *The Country Beyond the Forests: Short Stories and Selected Poems*

www.kmrice.com

Join the adventure with K.M. Rice's newsletter!

**Coming soon**

*Priestess (Afterworld Book Two)*

Made in the USA
Middletown, DE
27 November 2022